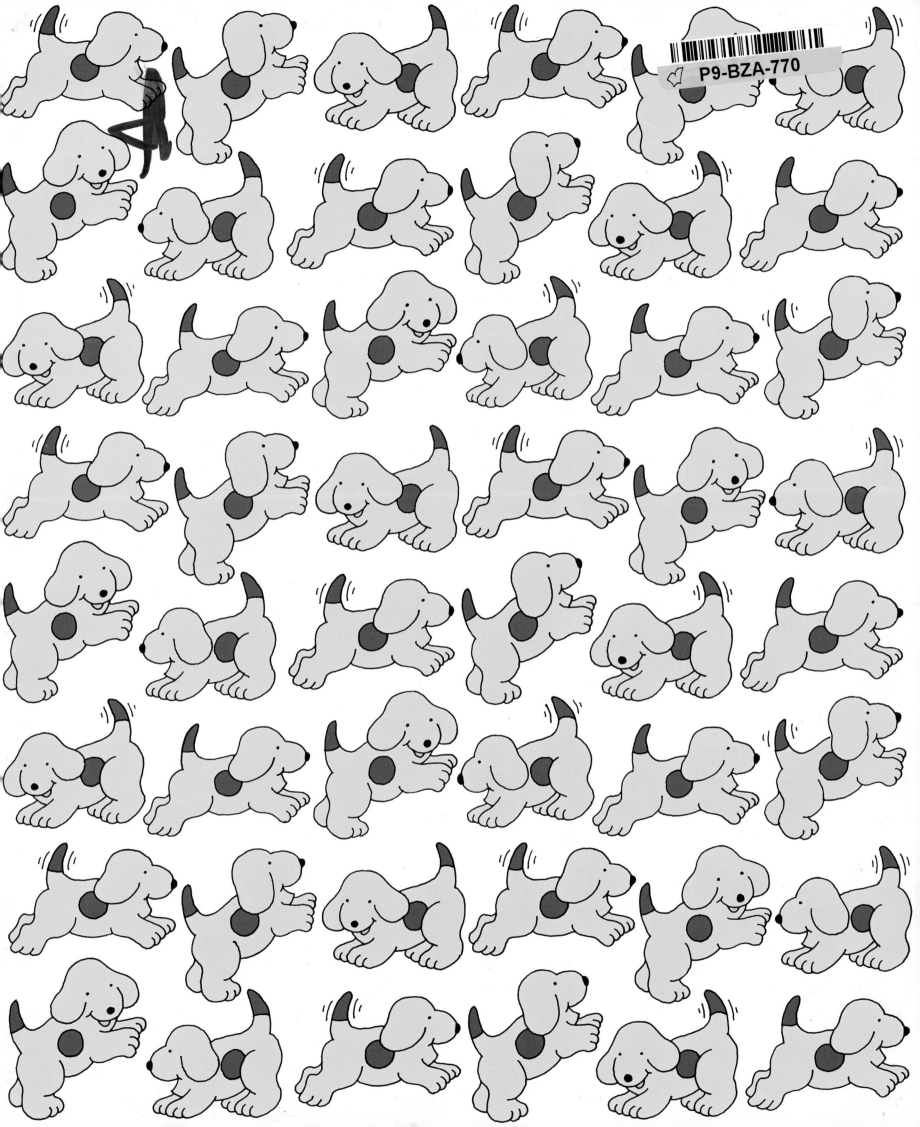

Spot's Big Learning Book

Spot's Big Learning Book

Eric Hill

G. P. Putnam's Sons • New York

Spot's Big Book of Words first published 1988.
Spot's Big Book of Colours, Shapes and Numbers
first published 1994.
This edition first published 1999.
First American edition, 2000.
Copyright © 1988, 1994, 1999 by Eric Hill.
All rights reserved.
Published simultaneously in Canada.
Planned and produced by Ventura Publishing, Ltd.,
27 Wrights Lane, London W8 5TZ, England.
Printed and bound in Singapore by Tien Wah Press (Pte) Ltd.
G. P. Putnam's Sons, 345 Hudson Street, New York, NY 100014.
G. P. Putnam's Sons, Reg. U.S. Pat. & Tm. Off.
L. C. number:
ISBN 0-14-056747-X
1 3 5 7 9 10 8 6 4 2

Spot's Colors, Shapes and Numbers

Colors: red

Spot is taking teddy for a ride in a red wagon. Helen is shopping with a red basket. The traffic light is red. What else on this page is red?

hat

fence

wagon

crayon

sailboat

apple

bow

notebook

basket

traffic light

bucket

yellow

Steve likes wearing his yellow raincoat and hat even when the rain has stopped. Tom has some yellow daffodils for his mom. What else on this page is yellow?

sun

rainhat

pencils

raincoat

lampshade

mug

FLOWER SHOP

sign

daffodils

bananas

lemon

green

bush

parrot

grass

frog

racing car

Helen is using a green watering can. Steve tries out his new green racing car. Watch out for the frog, Steve! What else on this page is green?

leaves

insect

watering can

planter

blue

socks

bird

jeans

T-shirt

sky

curtains

cap

book

brush

rocking chair

overalls

paint

Spot is sitting on his dad's blue rocking chair. Tom's dad is painting with blue paint. What else on this page is blue?

black

Tom just opened his black umbrella. He is wearing his black galoshes.
Some things are all black and some are black and white. Which are black and white?

giant panda

spider

blackbird

top hat

umbrella

cow

cat

galoshes

beetle

white

chalk

milk

dove

skirt

picket fence

newspaper

vanilla ice cream

Helen is wearing a new white skirt, and Spot is making a white snowman.
What else is white?

snowman

snowballs

snow

more colors

Spot looks pleased with his orange pumpkin. Tom is even more pleased with his basket of plums! Selina has never seen such a big strawberry-chocolate sundae, but it looks very yummy. Try some, Selina!

orange

purple

pink

brown

grey

What's this color?

What color is the tractor?
What color are the tires?
See how many colors you
recognize from the list at the
bottom of the page.

red	brown
blue	grey
green	black
yellow	purple
white	orange
pink	

Shapes: triangle

Spot's on the golf course, and his flag has a triangle shape. So has the tepee Steve is playing in.
We can see you, Steve! What else on this page has a triangle shape?

flag

roof

ice cream cone

beak

tepee

steeple

hat

square

Helen is playing on a square game board. Tom carries a square-shaped package. What else on this page has a square shape?

stamp

sandwich

game board

die

cushion

tablecloth

package

round

Spot looks at the world on a round globe. Helen plays with a round hoop – keep it rolling, Helen! What else on this page has a round shape?

sun

globe

watch

hoop

wheel

ball

drum

pizza

rectangle

book

envelope

tray

door

domino

picture
frame

suitcase

box

Steve is dressed up as
a bellhop. The suitcase has
a rectangle shape and so
does the envelope.
Tom is looking through an
empty picture frame.
What else on this page
has a rectangle shape?

diamond

Steve is flying a diamond-shaped kite. Helen is knitting a sock with a diamond pattern. What else on this page has a diamond shape?

kite

diamond ring

window pane

wire fence

road sign

sock pattern

oval

Tom is sitting at an oval-shaped table. Spot's mirror has an oval shape. What else on this page has an oval shape?

egg

eye glasses

table

spoon

tennis racket

platter

mirror

Easter egg

more shapes

Spot can see a crescent moon and two stars.
Helen holds a valentine card with a heart
on the cover. Who is it from, Helen?
The window has a curve at the top.
The arrow points the way.
A ruler has a straight edge for
drawing straight lines. The wavy
worm wiggles its way home. There
are many different kinds of shapes.

curve

star

crescent

wavy

straight

arrow

heart

What's this shape?

These are shapes you have seen before. Check them with the list at the bottom of the page.

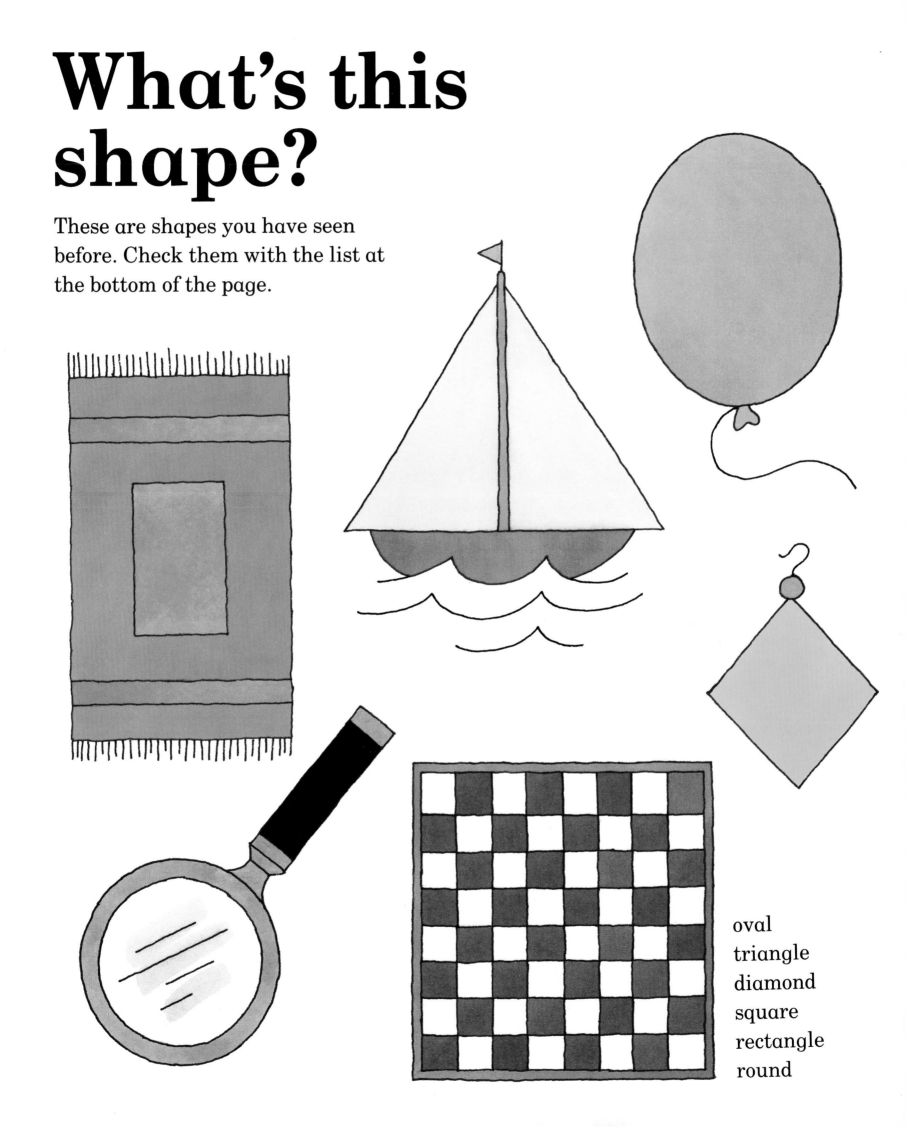

oval
triangle
diamond
square
rectangle
round

Numbers

Follow Spot and his friends as
they count from one to ten.
Go for it, Spot!

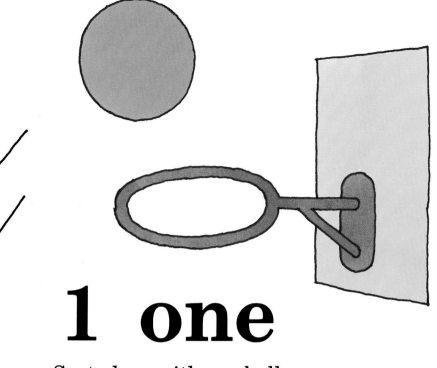

1 one

Spot plays with one ball.

2 two

Helen's bicycle has
two wheels.

3 three

Tom is balancing
three blocks.

4 four

Steve has four balloons.

8 eight

Tom can see eight butterflies.

9 nine

Steve counts nine ladybugs.

10 ten

Spot has ten books.

1 one   **2** two   **3** three   **4** four   **5** five

How many?

How many bones does Spot have?
How many rings does Tom have?
How many balls does Helen have?
How many marbles does Steve have?

6 six   7 seven   8 eight   9 nine   10 ten

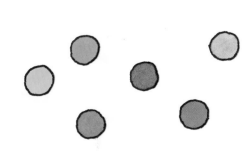

answers
four bones
five rings
three balls
seven marbles

freezer

✳ ✳ ✳

magnets

pitcher

orange
juice

coffeepot

refrigerator

coffee

toast

spoon

toaster

It's breakfast time
and Spot gets the orange
juice from the refrigerator.
Sally is making cheese
sandwiches for Sam to take
to work.

cereal

milk pitcher

bowl

mug

kettle

curtains

window

saucepan

strainer

frying pan

THE NEWS

teapot

plate

eggs

honey

knife

fork

bread knife

tablecloth

stove

cheese

bread

burner

mustard

sandwich

margarine

chimney

roof

farmhouse

sheep

fields

fence

orchard

truck

goose

Spot is helping his dad
on the farm. Tom and Helen
came along to help, but playing
with the wheelbarrow
is more fun.

horn

wheelbarrow

pond

duck

rope

ducklings

stake

frog

hoof

weather vane

dove

horseshoe

horse

barn

wheel

mouse

hay

stable

trailer

tractor

cow

cat

chicken

tail

rooster

milk
pail

milk can

pig

clock

blackboard

chalk

teacher

book

bookcase

Spot is at school.
Tom is coloring a picture
with crayons and Spot
and Helen are painting
pictures on their easels.
Soon they will all go
outside to play.

building
blocks

ruler

paste

scissors

pencil

eraser

workbook

desk

book bag

crayons

bell

map

slide

swing

seesaw

playground

door

lunch box

thermos

faucet

sink

easel

paper

brush

drip

apron

water jar

red

green

paint box

thumbtack

blue

yellow

keyboard

piano

Miss Bear's class is having a music lesson.
Spot thinks it's all great fun – what a noise they're making!

note

guitar

bow

violin

sheet music

harmonica

music stand

triangle

tambourine

recorder

Next door, Helen and Betsy are having a dance lesson. The teacher is going to play some ballet music on the stereo.

record

stereo

stereo speaker

Swan Lake

record cover

stage

steps

star

wand

spotlight

wings

barre

tutu

fairy costume

ballet shoes

cassette player

tape

Tom is painting the shed while Spot waters the vegetable seeds he has planted. Helen has picked some flowers to take home to her mother.

wall

hedge

gate

bush

path

apple tree

worm

leaf

buttercup

apple

butterfly

lawn

flowers

birdbath

flower bed

basket

shed

roof

brush

shears

window

hammer

shovel

door

fence

paint

hose

rake

bench

flower pot

carrot

pea

snail

fork

onion

trowel

watering can

earth

vegetable patch

seed packet

cabbage

potato

seagull

airplane

rod

Spot is at the beach and can't wait to get to the sea! Helen, Steve and Tom are at the beach, too. What is Helen looking at through her telescope?

float

line

pier

hook

seaweed

yacht

waves

hat

fish

surf

telescope

rubber ring

bucket

stairs

anchor

pebbles

suntan lotion

beach bag

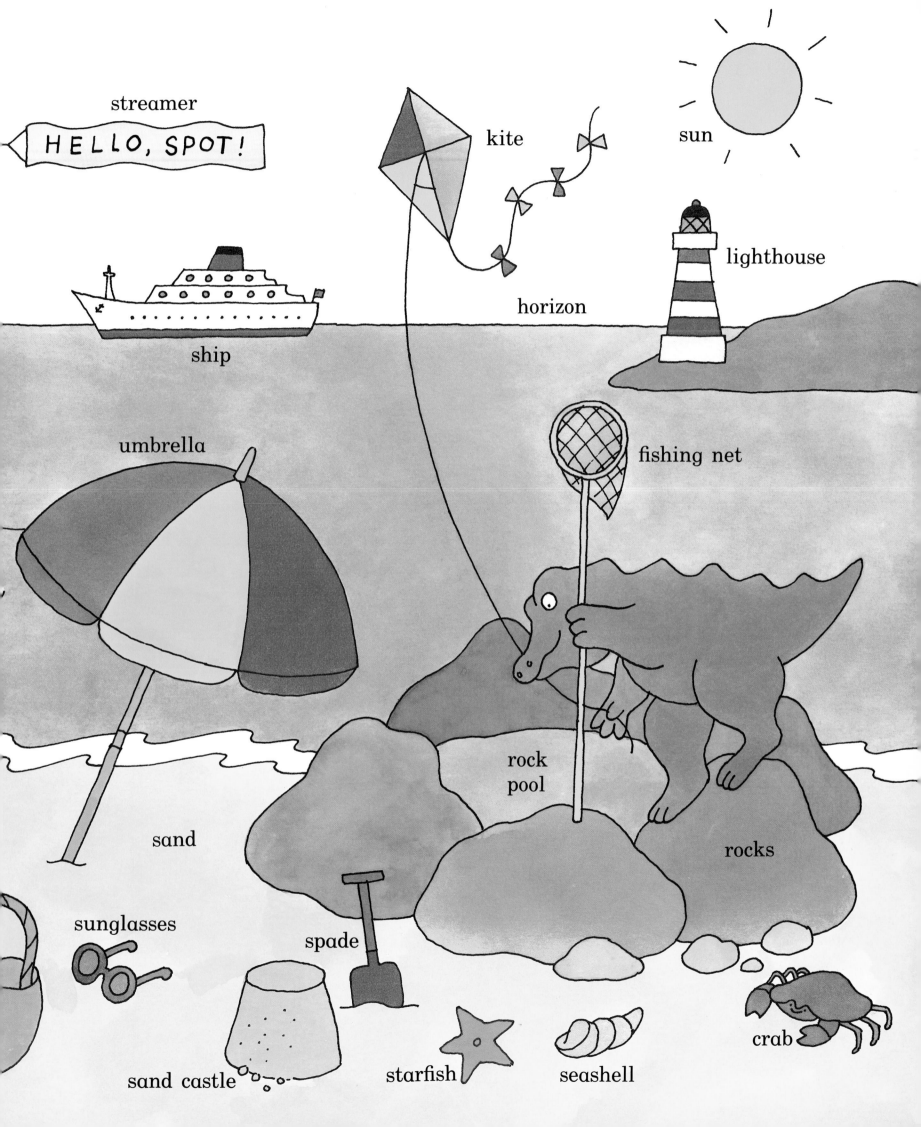

It's such a fine day! Everyone
is out in the park. Look at
Tom on his new bicycle!

tennis
ball

sun
visor

tennis
racket

net

roller skates

cap

jump rope

hand
brake

handlebars

pedal

tire

bicycle

helmet

elbow pad

knee pad

skateboard

headband

earphone

stopwatch

jogging suit

transistor radio

sole

sock

jogging shoes

heel

trampoline

tricycle

It's Spot's birthday and he has invited his friends to a birthday party. How old do you think Spot is today? Count the candles on the cake!

Happy bir

party hat

horn

ice cream

sandwiches

cookies

sailboat

teddy bear

lid

box

airplane

closet

hanger

cupboard

belts

rail

jacket

skirt

blouse

T-shirt

shoes

party dress

jeans

mirror

purse

drawer

beads

sandal

dress

Helen's mother has
bought a new dress and
sweater for Helen.
Do you like pink?
Helen does!

box

sweater

cowboy boot

cap

jacket

tie

overalls

shorts

duffel bag

pants

moccasins

socks

rugby shirt

shirt

boots

rain hat

suitcase

sneakers

umbrella

swimsuit

Spot is helping Steve pack for a vacation. Steve can't find a pair of socks that match. Look under the drawer, Steve!

Spot and his friends are enjoying some winter fun. Helen made the snowman and his dog. Spot thinks the dog looks like him!

ski poles

goggles

ski boots

skis

mountains

fur hat

snowball

earmuffs

frozen pond

mittens

broom

pipe

snowman

scarf

ice skates

boots

snowdog

snow

smoke

chimney

tree

icicle

log cabin

woolly hat

snowflake

gloves

sled

robin

footprints

log

Spot is staying overnight
at Tom's house.
Tom wants Spot to share the
bunk bed, but Spot pretends
he is camping out in his
sleeping bag and sleeps on
the floor.
Sleep well, Spot!

calendar

MAY

S	M	T	W	T	F	S
1	2	3	4	5	6	7
8	9	10	11	12	13	14
15	16	17	18	19	20	21
22	23	24	25	26	27	28
29	30	31				

pajamas

bulletin board

clock

night table

sheet

blanket

slippers

bunk bed

ladder

pillow